Y0-ELL-603

THREE CHEERS FOR MOUSE MATH!

Albert Is NOT Scared: **An ILA/CBC Children's Choices Selection**

A Mousy Mess: **Mathical Honor Book** for PreK–K

Albert the Muffin-Maker: **Moonbeam Children's Book Awards Bronze Medalist**

Albert the Muffin-Maker: "An enjoyable, instructive story with humor, heart and a pair of adorable mice." —**Kirkus Reviews**

"The Mouse Math series is a great way to integrate math and literacy into your early childhood curriculum." —**Teaching Children Mathematics**

"These titles present basic concepts, thinking skills, and reading skills all wrapped up in engaging stories. . . . Not only do the adorable mice introduce math, but they also share lessons about helping others . . . and thinking about the best way to solve problems. Consider these books first purchases." —**School Library Journal**

The Mousier the Merrier!: "Melmon's tender cartoons seamlessly integrate the counting lesson into the narrative." —**Publishers Weekly**

For Sanford —L.H.H.

For Ellie —D.M.

Special thanks to Meg Susi for providing the
Fun Activities in the back of this book.

Copyright © 2022 by Astra Publishing House

All rights reserved. Copying or digitizing this book for storage, display, or distribution
in any other medium is strictly prohibited. For information about permission to reproduce
selections from this book, please contact permissions@astrapublishinghouse.com.

Library of Congress Cataloging-in-Publication Data

Names: Houran, Lori Haskins, author. | Melmon, Deborah, illustrator.
Title: Super zero / by Lori Haskins Houran ; illustrated by Deborah Melmon.
Description: First edition. | New York : Kane Press, an imprint of Astra Books for Young Readers, 2022. |
Series: Mouse math | Audience: Ages 4-7 | Summary: "In this math-themed Mouse Math title,
Albert is given the uniform number zero on his soccer team and is sure it is cursed when
he can't score any goals"—Provided by publisher.
Identifiers: LCCN 2021016267 (print) | LCCN 2021016268 (ebook) | ISBN 9781635925746 (hardcover) |
ISBN 9781635925753 (trade paperback) | ISBN 9781635925760 (ebook)
Subjects: CYAC: Zero (The number)—Fiction. | Arithmetic—Fiction. | Mice—Fiction.
Classification: LCC PZ7.H27645 Su 2022 (print) | LCC PZ7.H27645 (ebook) |
DDC [E]—dc23
LC record available at https://lccn.loc.gov/2021016267
LC ebook record available at https://lccn.loc.gov/2021016268

10 9 8 7 6 5 4 3 2 1

Kane Press
An imprint of Astra Books for Young Readers, a division of Astra Publishing House
kanepress.com
Printed in China

Mouse Math is a registered trademark of Astra Publishing House.

SUPER ZERO

by **Lori Haskins Houran** • Illustrated by **Deborah Melmon**

KANEPRESS

AN IMPRINT OF ASTRA BOOKS FOR YOUNG READERS

New York

"Okay, Pipsqueaks!" Coach Agnes called. "Time to get your uniforms!"

Albert's squeakball team made a circle around Coach Agnes.

Coach tossed the first shirt to Clara. It had the number 5 on the back. Leo got number 8. Emily got number 6.

Coach kept tossing until there was one shirt left. "Here you go, Albert," she said.

Albert caught his shirt. "How come I've got a letter instead of a number?" he wondered.

"What do you mean?" asked his big sister, Wanda.

"This shirt has the letter O on it," said Albert, holding it up.

Wanda smiled. "That's not an O. It's the number zero."

Zero is a number. It looks like this: 0

"Zero?" Albert scrunched his nose. "I don't remember that number when I was learning to count. How many fingers do I hold up for zero?"

"Well, none," Wanda said. "Zero isn't worth anything."

"Not worth anything! What a terrible number!" said Albert. "Coach, can I have a different shirt?"

"Sorry," Coach Agnes said. "That's the last one."

Zero is worth nothing.

Saturday was the first game of the season.

Albert ran down the field. He got the ball and kicked it to Leo. Leo made a goal!

"Great goal, Leo!" called Coach Agnes. "Nice assist, Albert!"

Later, when the game was almost over, Albert got the
ball again. He passed it to Clara. Clara scored!

"Another assist," Coach said. "Well done, Albert."

Albert was glad he had helped his teammates score.
But he wished he had scored, too.

On the way home, Albert and Wanda talked about the game.

"Leo got a goal. Clara, too," said Albert.

1 + 1 = 2
One goal plus one goal equals two goals.

He frowned. "I got zero. Just like my number. I didn't add to the score at all."

"Don't worry," said Wanda. "You'll get a goal next time."

2 + 0 = 2
Two goals plus zero goals is still two goals.
A number plus zero is the same number.

But the next game was just like the first. And the game after that. And the game after THAT, too!

Albert kept making assists, but he didn't get any goals. Not one.

"Zero goals. It's like I don't even count." Albert groaned.

5 + 0 = 5
3 + 0 = 3
10 + 0 = 10

15

The morning of the final game, Leo sat in Albert's kitchen. "Today is my last chance to score," Albert told him. "But how can I, with the number zero? It's cursed!"

"Maybe you can reverse the curse," said Leo. "Pretend it's a letter O after all."

"Nah," said Albert. "I'll just think it stands for, 'Oh, Albert didn't score—AGAIN.'"

"What if you make the zero into a smiley face?" Leo said.

"It's worth a try!" Albert ran and got his paint set.

"WAIT!" cried Wanda, walking into the kitchen. "What are you doing?"

Albert explained his plan.

"You guys are thinking about this all wrong," Wanda said. "Zero is awesome. It's a secret superhero. I'll show you."

Wanda got some paper. "Tell me the coolest number you know."

"One hundred!" said Albert. "It's the highest number I can count to."

"Here's what one hundred looks like." Wanda painted 100.

"Hey, it's got two zeros!" Leo said.

"One thousand is even cooler than one hundred," said Albert.

Wanda showed them 1,000.

"It's got three zeros!" Leo shouted.

"What about one MILLION?" Albert said.

Wanda started painting . . . and painting . . . and painting!

"Phew!" said Wanda at last. She put down the paintbrush.

"Look at all those zeros," Leo whispered.

"Zero helps make one hundred *and* one thousand *and* one million?" said Albert.

Wanda nodded. "Like I said, it's a secret superhero. I guess you could call it . . . Super Zero!"

"So zero *isn't* cursed." Albert's heart beat faster. *If there's no curse, I CAN score*, he thought. *And I WILL!*

"Let's get to the field!" he cried.

"Don't you want to get dressed first?" Wanda asked.

By itself, zero is worth nothing. But when it's part of a number "team," zero is important. Without zero, 100 or 1,000 or even 1,000,000 would just be 1.

The minute the game started, Albert raced into action—
and never stopped.

He blocked the ball. He stole
the ball. He kicked the ball.

Albert was amazing!

With three seconds to go, the ball flew at Albert. *BOP!*
He bounced it off his knee, right to Clara.

"What a pass!" yelled Coach Agnes.

Clara kicked the ball into the goal.
The Pipsqueaks won!

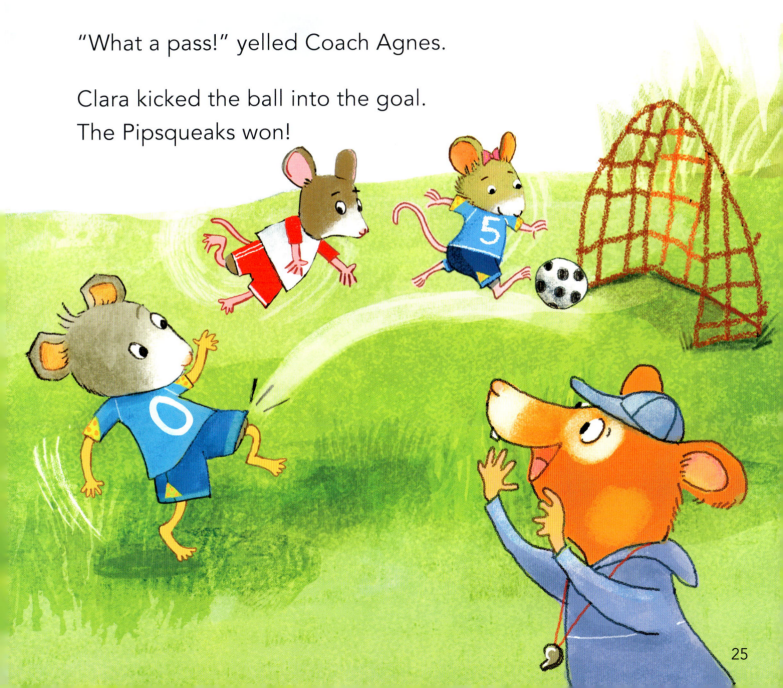

Albert's teammates jumped up and down, squeaking.
Albert was quiet.

"Aren't you excited?" Leo asked. "We're the champs!"

"Yes, but . . ." Albert looked at the ground.
"I still didn't score. And now it's too late."

The team headed to Cheesy Charlie's. Albert didn't feel like eating. Not even pizza.

"Terrific job, team!" said Coach Agnes. "Now for this year's Most Valuable Player. The award goes to . . ." She picked up a shiny trophy. "Albert!"

"WHAT?" cried Albert. "But I didn't score any goals. Zero!"

"Getting goals isn't all that matters," Coach said. "Over and over, you helped your teammates score. You set a record for the most assists!"

Leo gasped. "Albert, you were a secret superhero! Just like zero!"

"Yay, Albert!" the team cheered.

Albert grinned. "Coach, I know what number I want next year," he said. "SUPER ZERO!"

Super Zero supports an understanding of the concept of **zero**, both as a number and as a digit. Use the activities below to extend the math topic and reinforce children's early reading skills.

ENGAGE

▶ Read the title aloud. Ask children what they know about zero. Invite them to describe what zero would look like. They might show a closed fist with no fingers up. They might describe zero as an oval. Or they might describe zero as nothing, such as an empty plate or container.

▶ Examine the cover. Discuss the game being played. Invite children to share what they know about soccer.

▶ Ask them to make predictions about what will happen in the book. Invite them to give you a silent signal if their prediction happens during the story. You can pause to confirm predictions as you see children signaling.

LOOK BACK

▶ Review the pictures. Ask children to point out the numbers they notice on the players' jerseys.

▶ Ask: *If you were Albert's coach, what would you say to him? Why?*

▶ Ask: *What did Albert think about zero at the beginning of the story? How did his thinking change?*

▶ Reexamine the title after reading the story. Ask children to explain why the author chose that title for the book.

TRY THIS!

▶ Ask children to share numbers that have zeros in them, such as 40, 105, or 1,000. Write each number on a sticky note. Use a piece of string to create a number line.

Have children sequence them from least to greatest. Together, say each number aloud as it is sequenced. Then ask them to sort the numbers.

- Examples of ways children might suggest sorting:
  By the place of the zero in each number
  By how many zeros the number has
  By the total value of the number, such as more than 100 or less than 100

▶ When you add zero to any number, the sum is the same as the number you started with. Reinforce the concept of the identity property and prevent children developing the misconception that an additional digit is added to the number by playing a game of Simon Says Equations. Share some equations where one addend is 0 and ask children to act if the equation is true. Say: Simon says, "If __ + 0 = __, *touch your toes.*" Once they understand the game, they can lead it, sharing their own equations.

- Here are some equations to ask about:
  $40 + 0 = 40$ (True)
  $0 + 50 = 500$ (False)
  $99 + 0 = 99$ (True)
  $105 + 0 = 1050$ (False)
  $2 + 0 = 20$ (False)

🐭 THINK!

▶ Ask students what number they would want on their jersey. Can they count to that number? Can they count that number of objects? How many digits are in that number? Are there any zeros?

▶ The other players on Albert's team wear the numbers 1, 2, 3, 4, 5, 6, 7, 8, and 9. If the whole team wanted a zero on their jersey now, too, what numbers would they have?

BONUS: Have students design a jersey. Sequence the jerseys numbers from least to greatest.

◆ FOR MORE ACTIVITIES ◆

visit www.kanepress.com